Gribich And Friends

TRIP TO

PLANET DOOG

Written by **Marcus Porus, Shirley Porus** and **Philip Lange**

Illustrated by **Steven Jay Porus**

doog PUBLISHING GROUP™

Library of Congress catalog card number: 95-92692
ISBN: 0-9646125-1-8

First Printing April 1996
10 9 8 7 6 5 4 3 2 1

[1. Childrens–Fiction 2. Space Travel–Fiction 3. Animals–Fiction]

This book is environmentally friendly.

Printed on recycled paper utilizing soy based inks.
Printed in the United States of America.

Gribich and his friends teach such wonderful lessons to children in such an entertaining fashion. The books are exciting, well written and beautifully illustrated. However, equally as important, they give the children role models to follow and morals to learn. This is just the kind of book that we in education love to use with our children in discussions and in conflict resolution. I am looking forward to additions to this series."

Sharon J. Haddy, Principal
Norco Elementary School
Norco, California

It was a beautiful day. The sun shone brightly as Cabot Rabbit and Burl Squirrel walked through the forest. They came to a clearing, and Cabot looked up.

"Look Burl, do you see that?" she said. "It looks like a string of beads in the sky."

Burl answered, "Could that be Gribich? It *is* Gribich! He's come back!"

Gribich was their friend from Planet Doog. He had visited once before, and had promised to return. He said he would bring them to visit Doog. But Burl, Cabot and their friends couldn't all fit inside one spaceship, so this time, Gribich brought a ship for each of them. They were tied together like a train, and Gribich's spaceship pulled them all.

Cabot and Burl ran into the forest to find
their friends Bobbin Robin and Poof Wolf.
Cabot panted, "Come on, Gribich is here!
Gribich is here! We're going to Doog!"

The four animals ran back
to the clearing. They watched
the spaceships get *bigger*
and bigger as the ships
floated down to Earth. When
they landed, all the hatches
popped open. Gribich jumped
out of the first ship. He blinked
his big eyes, smiled his wonderful smile and called
out, "Hello o o o, hello o o o everyone. I'm back!"
The animals greeted him with shouts of joy.

Gribich said, "Pick a ship and climb in. We'll have a Doogle adventure!"

The animals climbed aboard and buckled up. The hatches closed with a hisssss.... four, three, two, one, blastoff!

Further and further from Earth they flew. The stars and planets glittered brightly in dark space. Poof said, "I wonder which planet is Doog?" Gribich pointed to a little green planet with two suns. "There it is," he said.

Down through the clouds
they flew, and landed on
Doog. Three Doogles had
come to greet them. Gribich
introduced everyone.

"This is Tuni. Her hearing is very good," Gribich said. Tuni replied, "I can hear your hearts beating."

Gribich continued, "This is Serky. She has wonderful eyesight." Serky added, "I'm good at finding things that are lost."

"And this is Falo," said Gribich. "He has a big, loud voice. He can also toot his horn. He warns us when there's trouble, and helps us celebrate when good things happen." Falo smiled and said, "I can be heard far away in the mountains."

"We'll show you Doog Forest," Gribich said. Poof and Bobbin were eager to explore, but Burl and Cabot weren't so sure. They walked close together and lagged behind the others.

Burl whispered, "Those Doogles scare me. And I don't like loud noises. I hope Falo doesn't blow that horn on his head."

"Shhhh," Cabot replied. "Tuni can hear you."

Burl continued, "I feel like Serky is watching us. I don't like it."

"Me either," Cabot said.

Along the path they met another
Doogle. "This is Moko," Gribich told
the animals. "He is a very good scout.
He knows the forest better than anyone."

"It's great to meet you," Bobbin chirped. "Will
you come with us?" Moko agreed, so they all
continued down the path together.

Poof was having a great time. He liked Tuni and walked beside her. She told him how happy she was on Doog, and said, "I hope you like it here, too. We'd be glad if you could stay awhile." Poof giggled shyly. "I hope so," he replied.

Bobbin flew beside Gribich and sang, "Thanks for bringing us to Doog!"

As they walked through Doog Forest, they saw many beautiful trees. Some had fruits and nuts just like trees on Earth. Others were very strange. Gribich pointed to some trees with trunks that twisted round and round and round. On top of each was a large ball with nothing inside.

"We Doogles sleep inside those balls at night," Gribich explained. "It's warm and cozy there. You can sleep in these trees too, if you want." Bobbin loved the idea. Poof said he preferred to sleep on the ground.

Gribich turned to the animals and said, "You can explore Doog Forest all you want. But please don't go into the reeds at the edge of the forest. The Canyon of the Winds is on the other side. The winds there are so strong they knock down trees. They blow huge holes through the mountains. It's only safe to walk through the canyon on one day every year. Tomorrow is that day. The winds will blow softly through the reeds and the holes in the mountains. They will make the most beautiful music in the galaxy. We call it our Festival of Music. You're all invited to join the celebration."

Poof and Bobbin could hardly
wait. Cabot and Burl
thought they had
a better idea.

Cabot whispered,
"Those Doogles are
scared of a little wind?
Not me! Let's go see
the canyon and hear
the music now." Burl
smiled, "Yeah, let's
go!" They waited until the others were far ahead,
then ducked into the reeds.

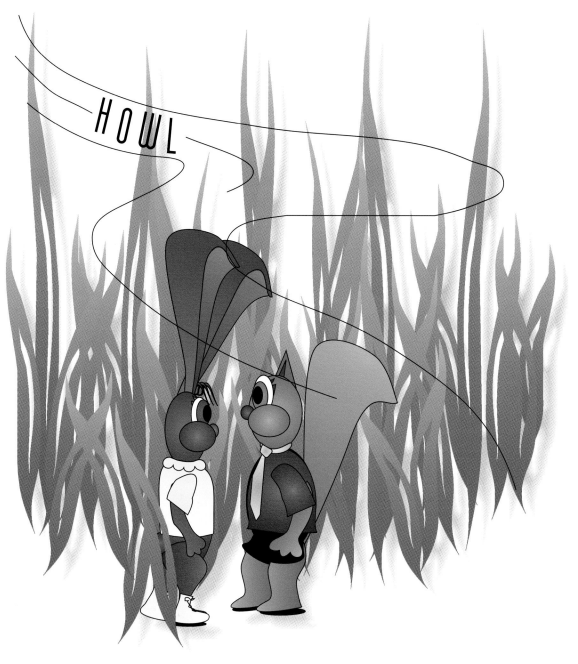

They had hardly gone ten paces when they began to hear a distant howling. "Do you think that's the music Gribich told us about?" Burl asked.

"Yuck!" Cabot said. "That doesn't sound like music to me! If that's the Doogles' idea of music, we aren't going to have much fun at the Festival tomorrow."

Suddenly, a gust of wind scooped them up and sent them tumbling over the reed-tops. The wind carried them far from their friends, and dropped them down hard. Thump, bump!

"Where are we?" Burl cried. Cabot whimpered, "I don't know. Maybe we should stay here until someone finds us."

Meanwhile, back on the path, Poof looked behind him and noticed that his friends were gone. He turned to Tuni and asked, "Where are Cabot and Burl?"

"I don't see them," she said.

Poof and Bobbin started to worry. Moko said, "I'm sure we'll find them. Tuni, listen carefully. Maybe they're calling us. Serky, you can be our lookout. Falo, you can call them with your big voice." The team of Doogles headed into the reeds. Gribich, Bobbin and Poof waited on the path.

In a thunderous voice, Falo shouted, "Cabot, Burl, where *are* you? Can you hear me?" Serky looked far and wide. Tuni put her ear to the ground and listened for the sound of footsteps. Moko sniffed the air and scouted for clues.

Cabot, Burl....

After a few tense minutes, Falo shouted, "We found them!" He blew his horn:

AH-OOO-GA!

AH-OOO-GA!

Moko led everyone back to the path. Gribich asked, "Are you ok? We were all worried about you." Cabot sniffled, "Yeah, we're fine now. But we were really scared."

"I'm glad you weren't hurt," Gribich said, "but why did you go into the reeds after I warned you not to?"

Cabot answered, "We just wanted to. We're sorry."

"We'd be in big trouble if you hadn't found us," Burl said in a small voice. "The wind was really strong."

As the group headed back into the forest, Burl whispered to Cabot. "Well, I thought the Doogles were weird at first, but I'm sure glad Tuni heard us and Moko found our tracks."

"Yeah," Cabot said, " Serky saw us through the reeds and Falo's horn is great too!"

It was getting late, so they all went to bed. The next morning, Cabot yawned and stretched. "I slept as well as I do on Earth," she said. "What's for breakfast?"

"Doogle nuts and Doogle berries," Gribich
replied. They were delicious!

After breakfast, everyone skipped toward the Canyon of the Winds. The wind blew softly and smelled like popcorn. The Earth animals and the Doogles stood at the canyon's edge and listened. The winds flowed around the reeds and through the mountains' tunnels and caves.

"It's the most beautiful music I've ever heard,"
Bobbin said. Cabot agreed: "This is really *cool*.
I'm glad I came to Doog."

Burl shouted, "Look everyone, do you see what I see? That mountain over there has a face — and it's smiling!"

"Wow," Poof said. Gribich laughed, "I wanted to surprise you. That mountain is the oldest Doogle. She is welcoming all of you to our home."

In the afternoon, the winds grew louder and stronger. They sounded less like music, and more like a lonely howl. It was time to leave the canyon.

Everyone laughed and played as they headed back toward the spaceships. The animals climbed aboard and waved goodbye.

"Come visit us again," the Doogles said. "We will," the animals called. As the hatches closed, Burl and Cabot cried, "We'll miss you!"

With a great rumble and snort, Gribich's spaceship blasted off, pulling the other spaceships behind. Whooooooosh! They were on their way home.

The End . . . until next time!

We would like to acknowledge
Shannon Hickey
for her editorial direction.

We would also like to thank
Elena A Escalera, Ph.D
Melanie Sandberg
Shoshana Phoenixx
for their editorial contributions.